Roadsigns

A Harey Race with a Tortoise

An Aesop Fable adapted by

Margery Cuyler

Illustrated by

Steve Haskamp

MARSHALL CAVENDISH CHILDREN

Library of Congress Cataloging-in-Publication Data
Cuyler, Margery.
[Road signs]
Roadsigns / by Margery Cuyler ; illustrated by Steve Haskamp.—1st Marshall Cavendish paperback ed.
p. cm.
Summary: Tortoise and Hare race along a road filled with traffic signs while the other animals cheer them on.
ISBN 978-0-7614-5306-2
[1. Traffic signs and signals—Fiction. 2. Racing—Fiction. 3. Turtles—Fiction. 4. Hares—Fiction. 5.
Animals—Fiction.] I. Haskamp, Steve, ill. II. Title.
PZ7.C997Ro 2008
[E]—dc22   2007014280

Text copyright © 2000 by Margery Cuyler
Illustrations copyright © 2000 by Steve Haskamp
All rights reserved
Marshall Cavendish Corporation, 99 White Plains Road, Tarrytown, New York 10591
www.marshallcavendish.us/kids
Creative Designer: Bretton Clark
Original hardcover book design by Billy Kelly
Letter art by Jessica Wolk-Stanley
The illustrations were rendered in acrylic paint on canvas.
Printed in China
First Marshall Cavendish paperback edition, 2008
Reprinted by arrangement with WinslowHouse International, Inc.

1 3 5 6 4 2

mc Marshall Cavendish
Children

To Diane, Brett, and Billy
—M.C.
For my family
—S.H.

Some signs in this book:

CURVE

DETOUR AHEAD

YIELD

DETOUR →

SLOW

SLOW DOWN

ROAD CONSTRUCTION 1000 FT

BRIDGE CLOSED

BLASTING ZONE 1000 FT

(rock being dynamited ahead)

PASS WITH CARE

EXIT

TUNNEL

CAUTION CHILDREN AT PLAY

END CONSTRUCTION

NO PARKING

FALLING ROCK

DANGER

SLIPPERY WHEN WET

(road is slippery when it rains)

ONE WAY →

PAVEMENT ENDS

NO PASSING IN TUNNEL

R X R

FLOOD AREA

DO NOT STOP ON TRACKS

ROAD CLOSED AHEAD

REST AREA ↗

ROAD MACHINERY AHEAD

KEEP LEFT

BUMP

STEEP HILL

DIP

10 M.P.H.

SCHOOL ZONE AHEAD

SOFT SHOULDER

STOP

TURN LIGHTS ON

SCHOOL BUS STOP

(no pavement on side of road)

One windy spring day, Hare challenged Tortoise to a race. Hare was sure that he would win, but would he?

READ THE SIGNS

AS YOU FOLLOW THE RACE. →

Tortoises Have Cute Knees
Go Hare!
START
Go HARE!
Bad Hare Day
Tortoise
Go Hare!
go tortoise

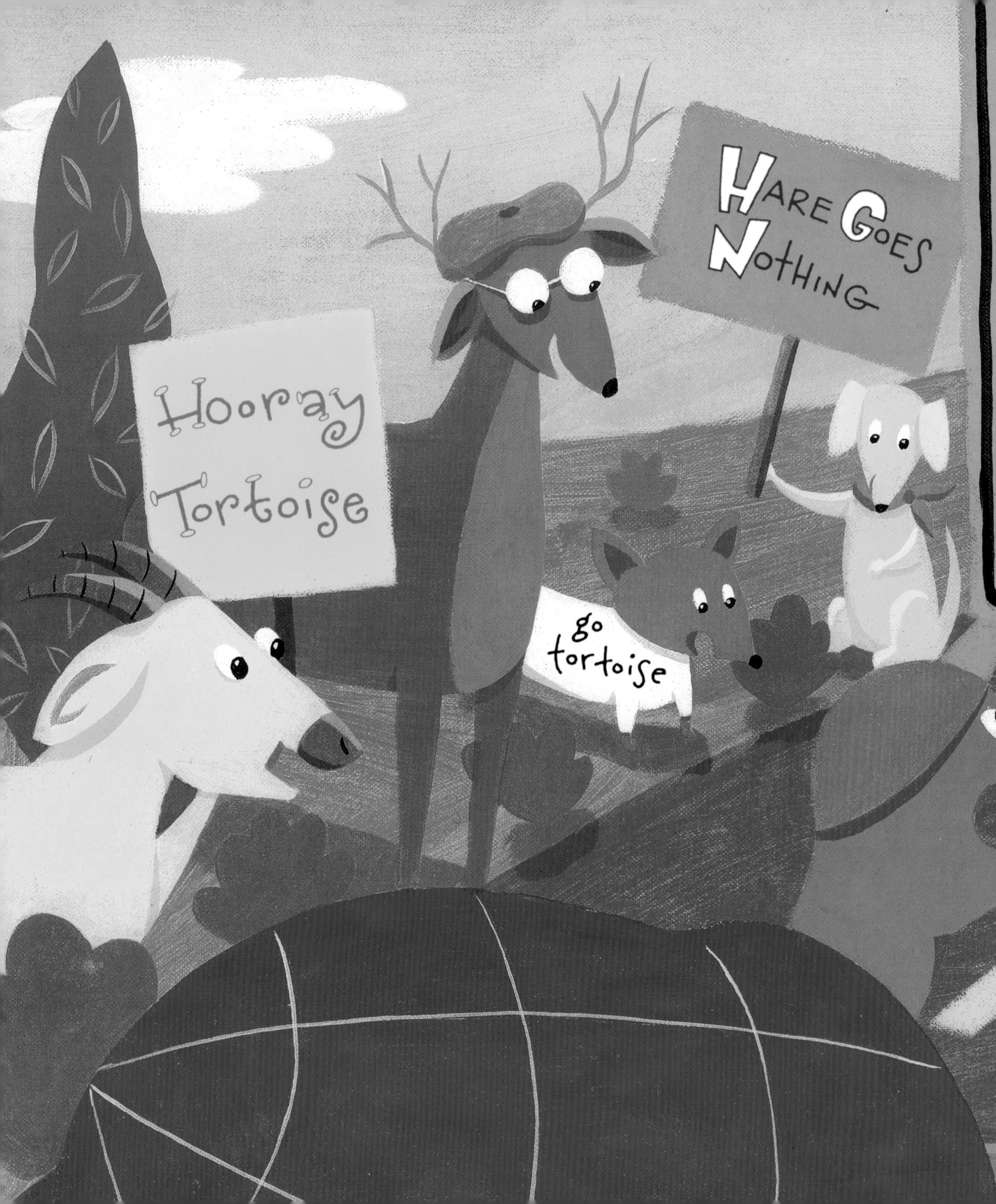

ROAD

AH

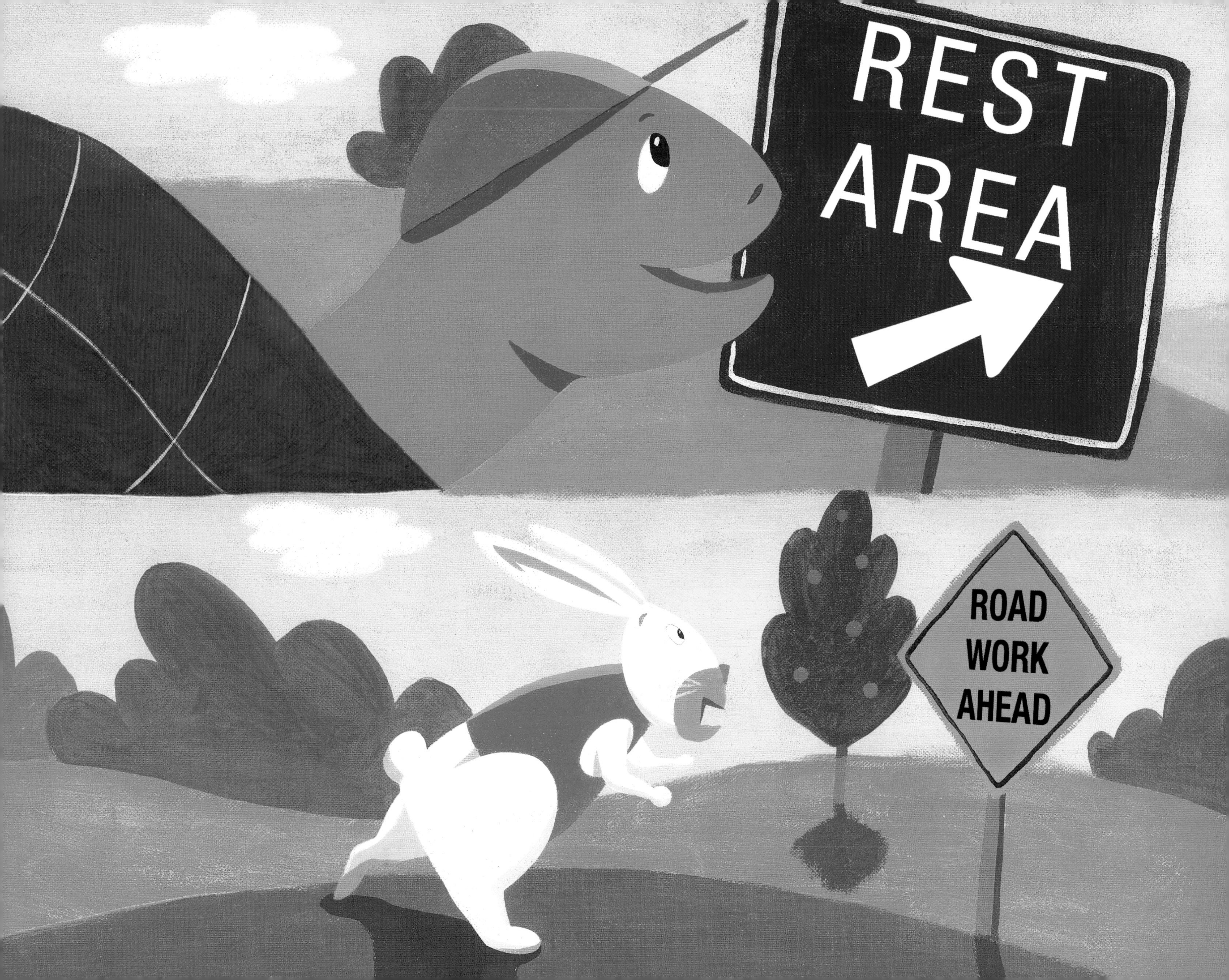
REST
AREA
ROAD
WORK
AHEAD

REST AREA

KEEP LEFT

go! go! go!

go tortoise

ROAD MACHINERY AHEAD

10 M.P.H.

DON'T DESPAIR, HARE!

REST ROOMS

PICNIC AREA

REST AREA →

Go Tortoise

ENTRANCE

50 M.P.H

CURVE

Tortoises
are
Smart

RxR

go
tortoise

DO NOT
STOP
ON
TRACKS

R R

Moral-Hard work pays off!
SCHOOL BUS STOP
Hooray Tortoise
go tortoise
Tortoise WINS
Bad Hare Day
FINISH
GO HARE